Ella's Bath

Peter Bently

QED Publishing

One **hot** day, Mum took Ella to the lake to cool off.

"That's better!" said Ella as she slipped into the water.

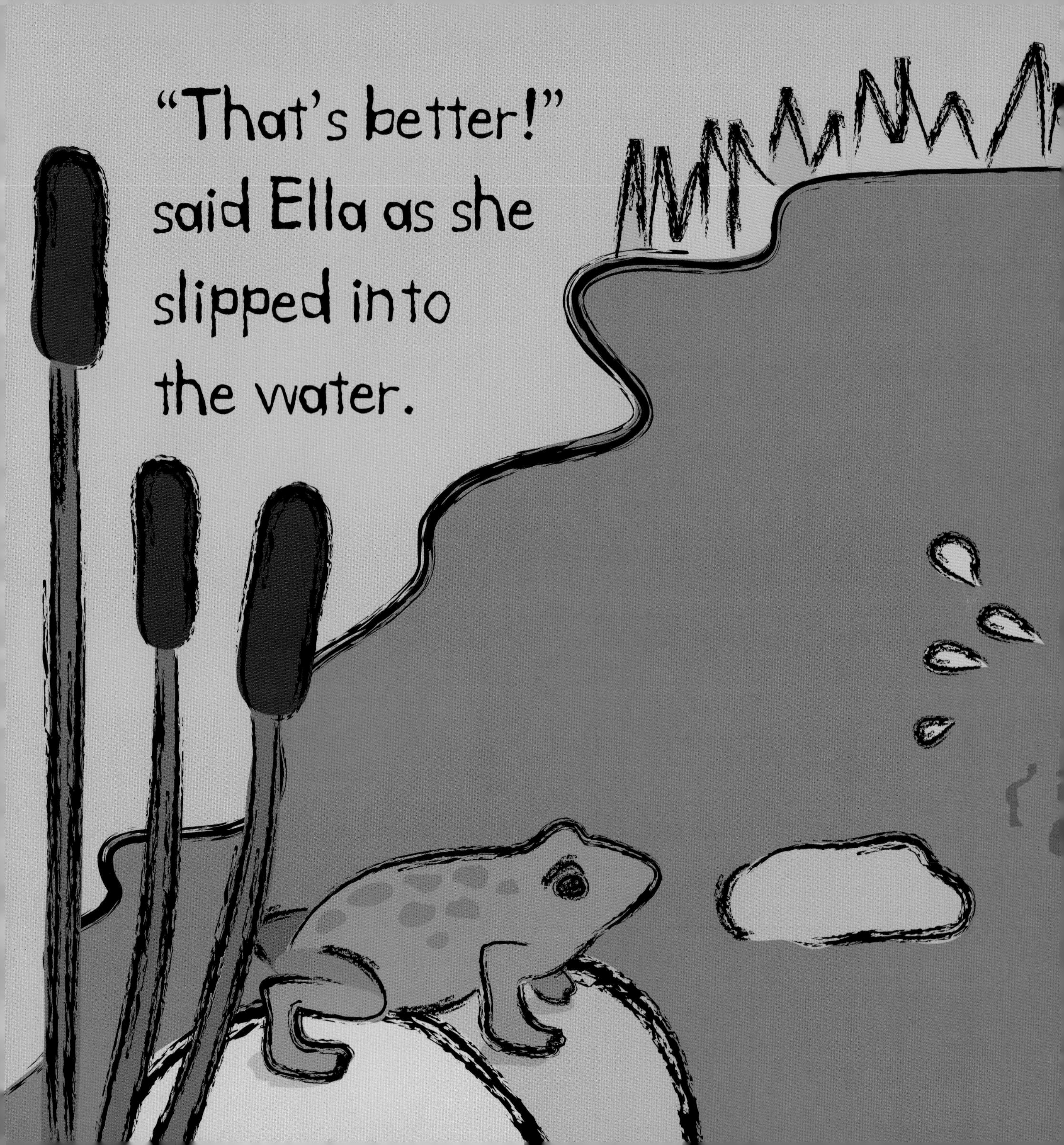

"It's lovely and cool."

Next, Ella played
chase with her brother.

"Caught you!"

she laughed.

"Now you're IT."

"**Phew!**" sighed Ella. "Now I'm all hot again."

"I know," she thought. "I'll break off a branch to make a fan."

Suddenly,
Stork flew down and snatched Ella's branch.

"Mum! Mum!"

yelled Ella. "Come quickly! Stork took my branch!"

"Don't worry,"
said Mum.
"I know an old trick."
And she whispered
something in Ella's ear.

"I bet I can make a bigger noise than you," said Ella.

And she lifted her trunk and trumpeted as loudly as she could:

"Root-i-toot!"

Stork frowned. He opened
his bill and went

"Crarrrk!"

even more loudly —
and dropped the branch.

Ella chuckled.
    Mum's trick had worked!

But Stork had
dropped the branch
into a mudpool.

Ella searched
and searched
but couldn't find
it anywhere.

"Never mind," she thought. "This mud is **lovely** and **COOL!**"

"Hey, Mum!" called Ella. "I think mudpools are great for cooling off!"

"And I think you need another **bath,**" laughed Mum.

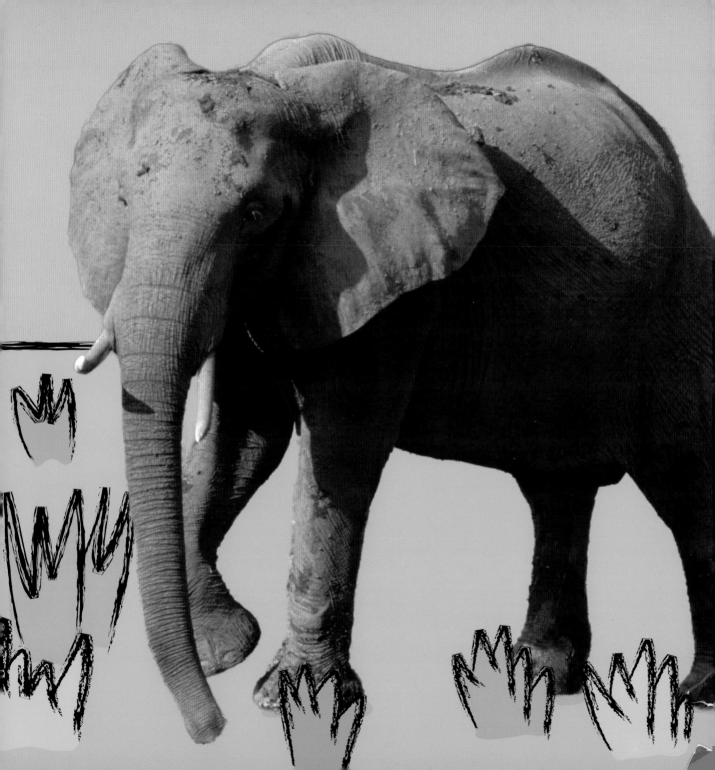

So Mum and Ella went for a swim.

"Snorkelling is fun!" thought Ella.

Notes for parents and teachers

- Before reading this book with children, look at the cover and see if they can guess what the story is about.

- Read the story aloud to the child or children. Encourage them to join in with any animal noises. Can they guess what happens in the end? Which pictures do they like best?

- In the story, Ella tries several ways to cool off. How many ways can the children count? Ask the children to explain, in their own words, how Ella tricks Stork.

- Have the children ever seen a real elephant? Discuss the differences between African and Indian elephants and where they live.

- Make the story of Ella and Stork into a play. One child can be Ella and two others can play her mum and Stork. The other children can be all sorts of other jungle animals. How do these creatures move?

- Ask the children to draw and colour in a jungle scene with Ella in it. They can make it as bright and colourful as they like.

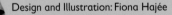

Design and Illustration: Fiona Hajée

Copyright © QED Publishing 2011

First published in the UK in 2011 by
QED Publishing
A Quarto Group company
226 City Road
London EC1V 2TT

www.qed-publishing.co.uk

A catalogue record for this book is available from the British Library.

ISBN 978 1 84835 647 4

Printed in China

Picture credits
FLPA front cover ZSSD/Minden Pictures, 1 Terry Whittaker, 2–3 Tim Fitzharris/Minden Pictures, 5 Gerry Ellis/Minden Pictures, 6–7, 14, 21 Ariadne Can Zandenbergen, 8–9 Andrew Forsyth, 11 Suzi Eszterhas/Minden Pictures, 12 Mitsuaki Iwago, 13 Imagebroker, 17 Shem Compion, 18–19 Frans Lanting, 20 Andrew Parkinson, 22–23 Rochard Du Toit/Minden Pictures, 24 Winfried Wisniewski/FN/Minden. **Shutterstock** back cover Four Oaks.